Twins' Night Before Christmas

Tobias and Timothy

written by
Cynthia F. Panks

illustrated by
Catherine Suvorova

To my twin granddaughters ~
Madison and Mackenzi
and
Sydney and Shelby

STORYBOOK GENIUS PUBLISHING
sbgpublishing.com

yip jar Book Design by yipjar.com

It's late Christmas Eve when this story begins,
in the home of Tobias and Timothy, twins.
Identical brothers, who look just the same, are
worried that Santa may not know their names!

Remembering their visit with Santa at the mall,
he knew their names just fine they recalled.

"Tobias, you are quite an athlete," Santa said.
"I like your fine medal that hangs by your bed.
And Timothy's trophy from his last recital...
you're quite a musician—there is no denial."

How did Santa do it? Did he just guess?
Twin identity crisis can cause so much stress.

If friends cannot do it, how does this elf
recognize each twin for his own unique self?

Momma says, "Santa's observant and smart."
But does he have the secret that tells twins apart?
Was he just lucky to get their names right?
Will he remember this Christmas Eve night?

The twins put on an early gift from Momma,
monogrammed names on plaid Christmas pajamas.

Christmas Eve was here and it was time for the test.
After all, he is Santa—he always knows best!

Tobias and Timothy made their big swap.
They kept the same bottoms and switched out the tops.

Ready to face Santa with a twin game,
Tobias wore Timothy. They swapped out their names!

As Momma and Dad slept, the boys quietly crept.
Underneath the bright tree, they would wait patiently.

Momma knew they were anxious so she'd understand!
And Dad said that Santa's a twin's biggest fan!

They waited for hours, not making a peep.
But before they saw Santa, they fell asleep!

When Santa arrived,
to his chagrin, he tripped,
he tumbled and almost
stepped on a twin!

"HO, HO, HO!
A twin slumber party under the tree?
That's a big NO—not on Christmas Eve!"

"This must be a scheme!
Twins should be in bed
having sugar-plum dreams."

Santa took one more look, so observant and wise.
He said, "I am not fooled by their pajama disguise!"

He placed presents for Timothy—and Tobias, too.
Santa knew he still had one last thing to do!
He sat down with a cookie and penned them a note.
Here are the wise words that dear Santa wrote.

Timothy and Tobias,

Twins are a gift to the world,
times two! But your real
blessings lie inside each of you.
Though you may look just alike,
you're set uniquely apart by
the actions and words that
represent separate hearts.
Although others may guess, be
true to yourself! Your face with
your name will outshine the rest!

Santa

The boys were awakened by paws on the roof.

Was that Santa leaving?

Did they miss their proof?

The note Santa left gave
their names a new light.

And they heard him exclaim as he drove out of sight.

"Celebrate being twins! Forget all the drama!
I know who you are, so switch back your pajamas!
Hop into bed and let this story end with a DOUBLE
Merry Christmas and goodnight to all twins!"

CPSIA information can be obtained
at www.ICGtesting.com
Printed in the USA
LVHW071648011121
702141LV00006B/241

9 781952 954658